The Best Trade of All

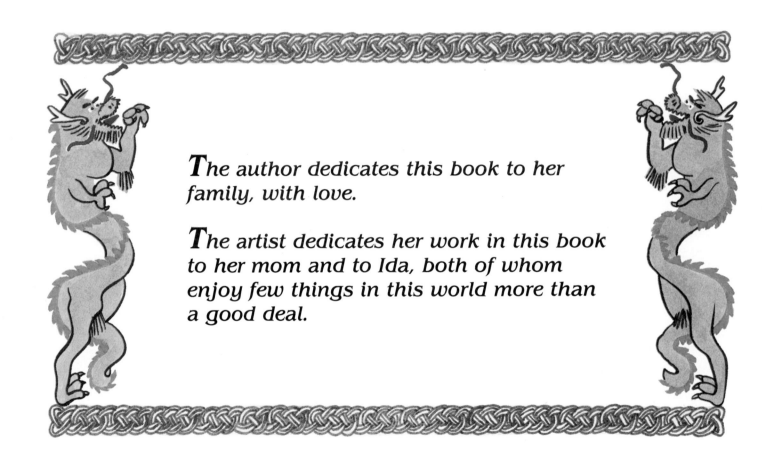

*T*he author dedicates this book to her family, with love.

*T*he artist dedicates her work in this book to her mom and to Ida, both of whom enjoy few things in this world more than a good deal.

Published by Raintree Publishers Inc., 205 West Highland Avenue, Milwaukee, Wisconsin 53203.

Art Direction: Su Lund

Printed in the United States of America.

1 2 3 4 5 6 7 8 9 0 87 86 85 84 83

Library of Congress Cataloging in Publication Data
Bourque, Nina.   The best trade of all.   "A Carnival Press book."
Summary: The trader Bevin and the shopkeeper Kumi, from two widely separated and very different lands, become partners and embark on a career of adventure and friendship. [1. Merchants—Fiction. 2. Friendship—Fiction]   I. Urbanovic, Jackie, ill.   II. Title.
PZ7.B6683Be   1983   (E)   83-7352   ISBN 0-940742-33-0

The Best Trade of All

Story by
Nina Bourque

Illustrations by
Jackie Urbanovic

A Carnival Press Book Raintree Publishers Inc.

In a village of rustling oak trees and sturdy log huts
lived a trader named Bevin.

Swirling oceans away, in a city of willow trees and open-air shops, lived a storekeeper named Kumi.

Bevin traveled the countryside trading her merchandise— sometimes rattling cooking pots and sometimes honking geese.

Kumi worked long hours selling her wares—some days crunchy rice cakes and some days chirping crickets in bamboo cages.

One morning Bevin swapped a herd of mooing cows and bleating lambs for a tall sailing ship.

"Yippee," she shouted.
"I'll load up all my goods
and have a rip-roaring
adventure!"

That same morning Kumi sold all of her
swishing scarves and all of her tinkling chimes.

"Hurray," she cheered. "I'll close my shop early
and leave this hurly-burly marketplace."

11

In her bumping cart, Kumi rode to the canal.

Plop! Plink!

She threw pebbles into the water
and dreamed of faraway lands.

"If only I could travel like
the traders who come to
my shop," she murmured.

Bevin's ship splashed through the ocean with her chattering animals and clattering cargo.

"Yahoo," she cried. "I'm a whiz at sailing! But I wish I had someone to sail with besides this babbling crew."

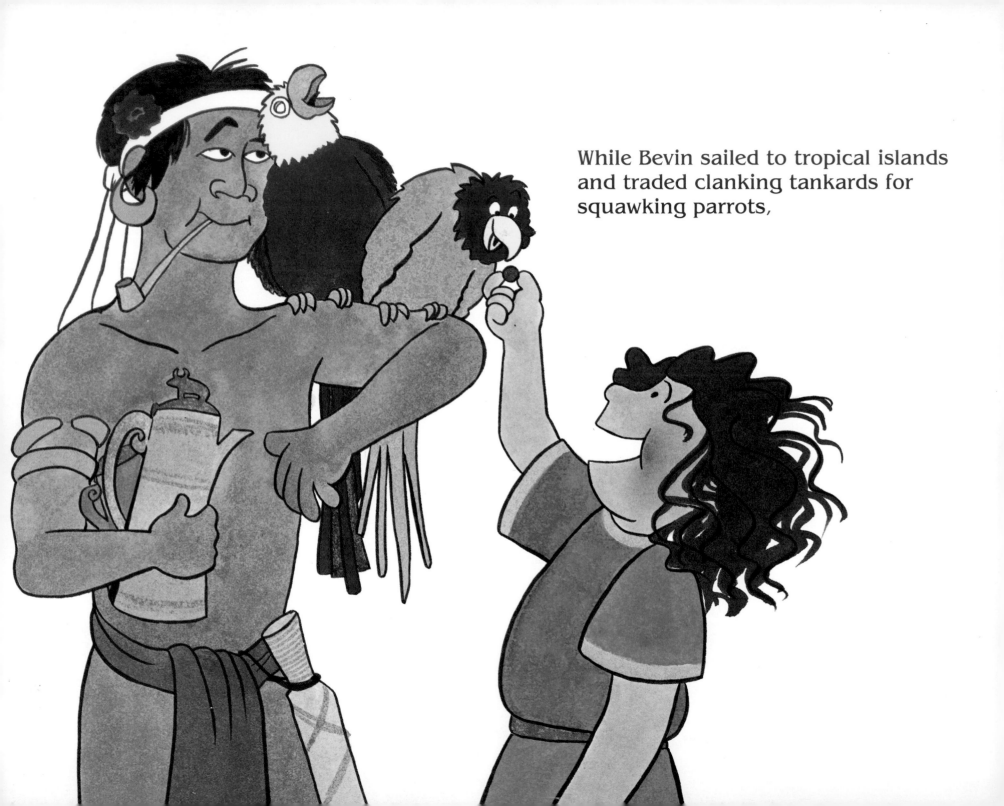

While Bevin sailed to tropical islands and traded clanking tankards for squawking parrots,

Kumi bought hissing snakes
and clucking chickens from
wandering peddlers.

One afternoon Bevin ran into a
terrible storm. Winds howled,
thunder boomed, and the ocean
swelled around her.

Her ship creaked and groaned, and the animals on board ran hurry-scurry to find shelter.

"We're topsy-turvy," blurted Bevin as she checked her soaking maps. "That storm snarled up our course."

For days the ship zigzagged until Bevin spotted land.

"Everything is humdrum," Kumi sighed as she sat by the canal. "Every day customers grumble, traders mumble, and I never see anything new."

Suddenly Kumi spotted Bevin's sailing ship. "Look out," she yelled. "Don't crash!"

Thump! Thud!

The ship docked.

"Land at last!" whooped Bevin, charging down the gangplank. "What country have I come to?"

"You're in a land of wondrous things," said Kumi, reaching into her cart. "The land of jingling bells, huffing dragons, and best of all—*fireworks!*"

BANG, SIZZLE, POP!

"Terrific!" said Bevin. "I'm from a land of screeching griffins, whining bagpipes, and clanging shields."

"I've got swooping kites and plinking samisens to trade," said Kumi.

"And I've got twanging lyres and clinking coins to swap," said Bevin.

Days of happy trading followed, and Bevin and Kumi
soon became partners. They rebuilt Bevin's ship and
stocked it well, from bow to stern.

"Here's to adventure!" Kumi shouted.

"And here's to friendship!" Bevin cheered as they sailed away together.

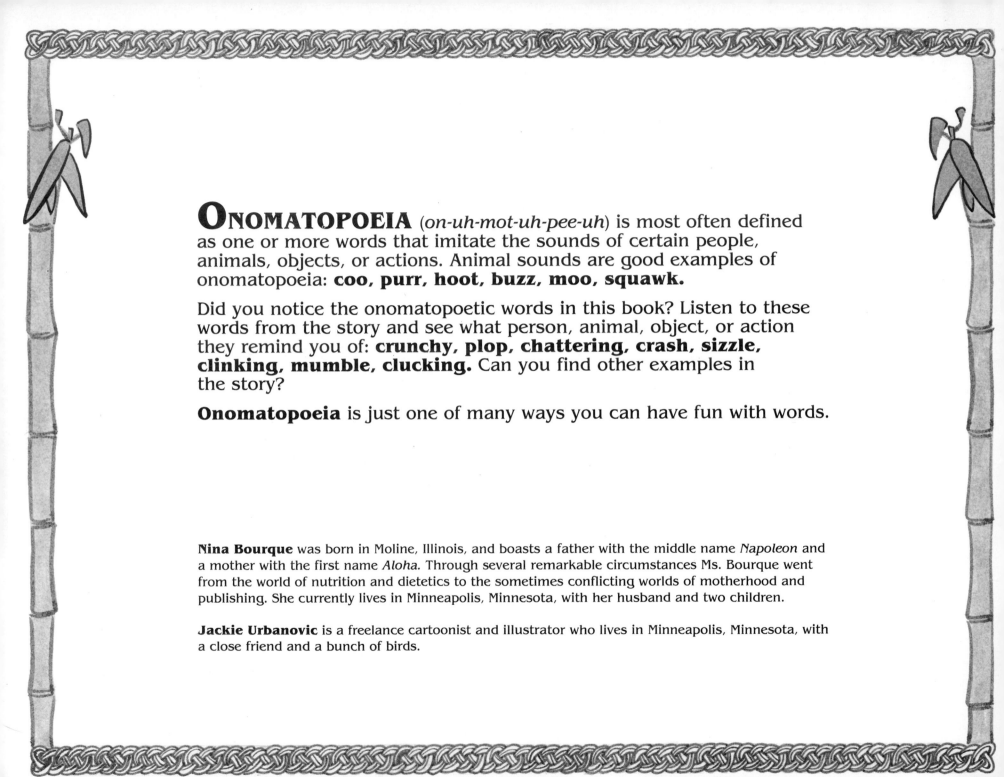

ONOMATOPOEIA (*on-uh-mot-uh-pee-uh*) is most often defined as one or more words that imitate the sounds of certain people, animals, objects, or actions. Animal sounds are good examples of onomatopoeia: **coo, purr, hoot, buzz, moo, squawk.**

Did you notice the onomatopoetic words in this book? Listen to these words from the story and see what person, animal, object, or action they remind you of: **crunchy, plop, chattering, crash, sizzle, clinking, mumble, clucking.** Can you find other examples in the story?

Onomatopoeia is just one of many ways you can have fun with words.

Nina Bourque was born in Moline, Illinois, and boasts a father with the middle name *Napoleon* and a mother with the first name *Aloha*. Through several remarkable circumstances Ms. Bourque went from the world of nutrition and dietetics to the sometimes conflicting worlds of motherhood and publishing. She currently lives in Minneapolis, Minnesota, with her husband and two children.

Jackie Urbanovic is a freelance cartoonist and illustrator who lives in Minneapolis, Minnesota, with a close friend and a bunch of birds.